Tad

Benji Davies

HarperCollins *Children's Books*

For all the small people who want to be big people.
Especially for Esther.

First published in hardback in Great Britain by HarperCollins *Children's Books* in 2019

10 9 8 7 6 5 4 3 2 1

ISBN: 978-0-00-821279-7

HarperCollins *Children's Books* is a division of HarperCollins*Publishers* Ltd.

Text and illustrations copyright © Benji Davies 2019

Visit our website at:
www.harpercollins.co.uk

Printed in China

Tad was a frog.
Well, that's not quite true –

she was almost a frog.

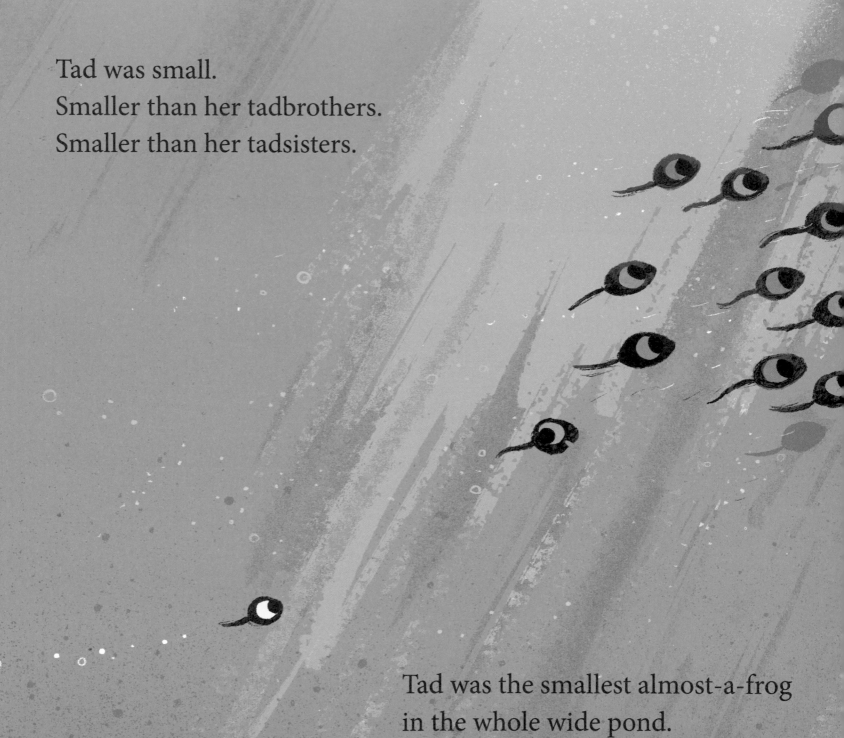

Tad was small.
Smaller than her tadbrothers.
Smaller than her tadsisters.

Tad was the smallest almost-a-frog
in the whole wide pond.

She was so small that she had to wiggle her tail
twice as fast as any of the others just to keep up.

"Keep up!" they would say. "Or Big Blub will get you!"

Tad had never seen Big Blub.
Big Blub, they said, was a

great,

big,

nasty,

fish.

Big Blub swam in the deep, dark, murky part of the pond.

He was as old as the mud, they said.

He would wait till the sun went in, till all the pond was grey, then he would glide out from the dark patches and …

GULP!

No, no – Tad did NOT want to know.
She decided to not believe in Big Blub.

But, just in case, she kept to the shallow, sunny parts of the pond
where Big Blub could not get her.

And when the sun went in she carefully hid behind the rocks and plants …

in hope that Big Blub would not find her.

Day by day, the tadpoles grew.

They grew back legs, then front legs.

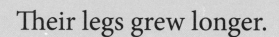

They grew webbed toes.

Their legs grew longer.

Their legs grew stronger.

Stretching their four legs as wide as they could, they felt like they wanted to climb out of the pond.

They rushed into the shallow water quicker than you or I can blink.

swoosh-wiggle-swish
swish-wiggle-swoosh

Their tails got smaller and smaller, until they no longer had tails at all.
"We've lost our tails! We've lost our tails!" they cheered.

All except for Tad.

Every night they would find a big
leaf and curl up together.

But as the nights passed
Tad noticed fewer and fewer
tadpoles to curl up with.

10 9 8 7 6

Each night Tad counted her tadbrothers
and tadsisters.

5 4 3

Where had they all gone?
She didn't like to think.

Tad played in the shallows with her last tadbrother and her last tadsister. "You can't catch us, Big Blub!" her last tadsister called out into the shadows.

But soon there were just two.
"It seems there are much fewer of us than before, don't you think?" said Tad to her last tadbrother.

And then there was only one.

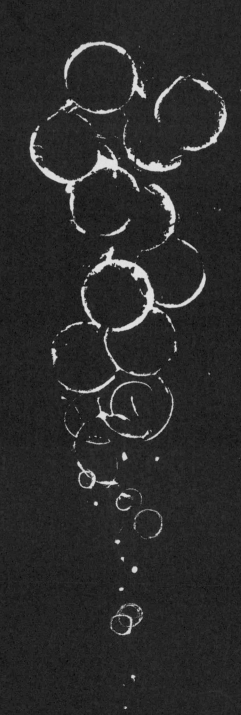

But she was strong and she was clever
and she knew all the best hiding places.

Big Blub would never catch her.

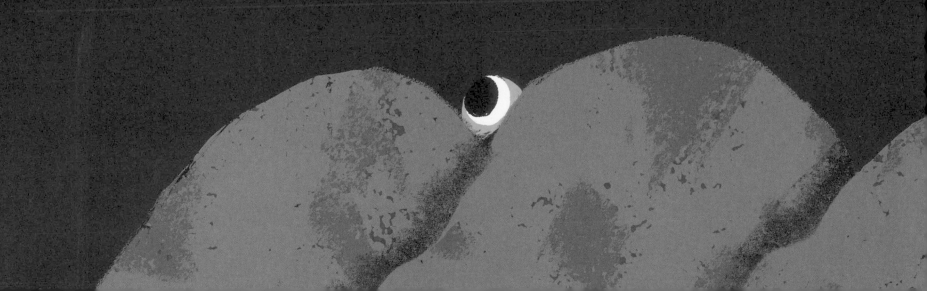

Oh no! Big Blub!

Tad swam faster than she had
ever swum before.

Then Tad did something
she had *never* done before.

and up and up.

and up…

She swam up…

Big Blub sank back to the bottom of the pond,
where he belonged, amongst the mud and ooze,
deep, dark and murky.

GLUGLUBLUGLUBLUB..blub..blub

Tad climbed up on to a rock,
her big round eyes blinking at
the bright sky. It felt good
to be out of the water.

"I've lost my tail!
I've lost my tail!"
she sang.

Tad was a frog.

She had a funny feeling, a twist in her belly,
spreading out to the ends of her toes.

She coiled up tight like a spring...

…and jumped.